I0640958

Firebrand Firestorm

The Ancestors of Bjorn Esterday

Volume 04

Seeking Truth

March & April 1776

Wynter Sommers

Wynter Sommers

Published by Pure Force Enterprises, Inc.
California, USA
Since 2002

INGRAM

INGRAM® Distribution

DEDICATION

To those who feel strongly about truth,
justice, and the integrity of America;
your honorable actions make us proud.
To those who wonder if their daily
choices matter; your small decisions
impact generations to come.
To those everyday people who don't think
they have what it takes; when you strive
for extraordinary things, the impossible
becomes reality.
Your dreams today become our future
tomorrow.
Thank you for everything you do.

Bjorn Esterday
Was Not Born Yesterday
Series

Firebrand (15 Volumes+Conversation Station Book)
Edges (9 Stories +Conversation Station Book)
Gone (18 Stories + Conversation Station Book)

Bjorn EDGES Series

EDGES Book 1-Swift Encounter
EDGES Book 2-Rousing Attack
EDGES Book 3-One Foot Under
EDGES Book 4-Earthshake
EDGES Book 5-Broken String
EDGES Book 6-Key Witness
EDGES Book 7-Who is She?
EDGES Book 8-Vanish
EDGES Book 9-Chase or Die

Bjorn Series Alternate Reading Plan

1st	Edges Book 1		22nd	Gone Book 10
2nd	Edges Book 2		23rd	Firebrand Vol 9
3rd	Gone Book 1		24rd	Gone Book 11
4th	Firebrand Vol 1		25th	Firebrand Vol 10
5th	Edges Book 3		26th	Gone Book 12
6th	Firebrand Vol 2		27th	Gone Book 13
7th	Gone Book 2		28th	Firebrand Vol 11
8th	Gone Book 3		29th	Gone Book 14
9th	Firebrand Vol 3		30th	Firebrand Vol 12
10th	Gone Book 4		31st	Gone Book 15
11th	Firebrand Vol 4		32nd	Firebrand Vol 13
12th	Gone Book 5		33rd	Gone Book 16
13th	Gone Book 6		34th	Firebrand Vol 14
14th	Edges Book 4		35th	Gone Book 17
15th	Firebrand Vol 5		36th	Firebrand Vol15 (End)
16th	Gone Book 7		37th	Gone Book 18 (End)
17th	Firebrand Vol 6		38th	Edges Book 5
18th	Gone Book 8		39th	Edges Book 6
19th	Firebrand Vol 7		40th	Edges Book 7
20th	Gone Book 9		41st	Edges Book 8
21st	Firebrand Vol 8		42nd	Edges Book 9(End)

ACKNOWLEDGMENTS

We acknowledge those who actively build peace. We acknowledge all the selfless talent which contributed to creating meaningful tokens of consideration and sharing. We acknowledge that every person has a daily choice of right or wrong... and we thank you for choosing the right, good, honorable path filled with integrity because that is the difficult and brave path. Small choices today become lasting monuments of loving hope tomorrow.

CONTENTS

0 PREFACE

Previously, we learned about Polly's voyage to the colonies and how she met her husband, Button. Meanwhile, Jane, Polly's new friend, wants to help Polly, but also has her own mission of justice she must pursue.

Although Jane is not able to personally care for this newly misplaced Irish pioneer, Jane did decide to find a place for Polly to recover and be cared for. Much like the Good Samaritan, Jane decided to be responsible for the care of this fellow pioneer even-though they are from very different classes. Jane persists in always trying to do the right thing because she herself has been victim to circumstances beyond her control which has resulted in a drastic reduction in Jane's own previously very comfortable lifestyle.

Jane, instead of being bitter, has decided to be empathetic to others who have fallen victim to circumstances beyond their control. Jane figures if she can reach out and help others even-though she can not offer as much aid as she might have back in England before her situation forced her to make a voyage to these colonies herself, she will do what she can with what little she has.

Did Jane do the right thing to make the decision to care for Polly in her condition? Will the Dunlaps welcome this Polly-stranger with the Irish borough and accent, which is often associated with a demographic which despises the English mistreatment of the Irish people?

1 CHAPTER 30: (FEB 1776) Mother Mulhoolin's Church Challenge

Mrs. Mulhoolin, Polly's mother, crept into the old Irish stone church right after mass started. She stood in the very back, where only those on the alter, such as the priest, could see her. After the priest gave his blessing at the end of mass, Mrs. Mulhoolin waited until the priest invited the congregation to bow their heads in prayer and then she quietly left.

She went outside to the small graveyard to visit her husband's head stone.

"Widowhood doesn't suit me, my love," She whispered softly to her husband's grave. "I've missed you these six years..." She turned to watch from a distance as the church doors opened allowing for the egress of the parishioners.

The priest shook hands with some, and bade farewell to all. When the last person smiled and said good bye, the priest leaned over to the nun standing next to him.

"Sister, that woman has been coming more often of late," he commented softly as he pointed at widow Mulhoolin out in the graveyard.

"Aye. She isn't catholic, but her husband was and so she comes to listen...I think to be close to her husband's memory," the nun replied.

"How long has she been doing this?" the priest asked.

The nun said, "Oh, you've been here for six months. Before he retired, Father

O'Leary had seen her come in every now and again for... I'd say..." the sister paused, "About five or six years, now. I hear her husband died during a slave raid. I'm not one to share gossip, Father, but the townsfolk say he loved her so much that after he and other village men were swept up, he fought to the death to escape so he could return to her side... however, they killed him. The widow's name is Mrs. Mulhoolin."

"Does Mrs. Mulhoolin wish to convert to *Catholicism*?" The priest asked.

"Oh, I'm not certain," the sister replied, "Sent her daughter to the Colonies in America that same year her husband died back in '70. I sometimes see her slip into the sanctuary when it is empty and she prays for her daughter. A while after her husband died, the village was attacked again by slave raiders and I understand her home was destroyed... so she's been staying with another widow here in this village for the past few years."

"And this is an agreeable situation for Mrs. Mulhoolin?" the priest asked.

"No," the nun shared, "the widow recently passed away and the widow's son has now claimed the house as his inheritance. He has given Mrs. Mulhoolin notice and she must soon leave."

"Has Mrs. Mulhoolin made other lodging arrangements?" The priest asked.

"I believe she is quite on her own with nowhere to go. She shared with one of the sisters who prayed for her that since she has not heard from her daughter, she prays for her soul as if she were dead."

"Is her daughter dead?" the priest asked.

She lglanced at the widow looking forlorn in the graveyard and replied to the priest, "I don't know what happened to her daughter. That poor Mrs. Mulhoolin. No family left here in Ireland. It was a risk sending the lass to those wild lands."

Mrs. Mulhoolin was staring at her husband's grave stone, facing away from the church and from the priest and nun.

"The Colonies, you say?" The priest asked.

"Yes. Father. On the American continent somewhere."

"Do you know of the sailor in our flock who has been to the Colonies?" the priest asked.

The nun thought about it a while and said, "Yes. A rare one who comes to mass and avoids the taverns. What of that sailor?"

"He told me," The priest started, "he sailed with *Captain Cook*, the British Explorer. He said that as early as this Summer, this Captain Cook is to depart again on an expedition to find a way to sail from the Eastern or Indian Ocean to the Western Ocean across the northern part of New World."

"Western Ocean?"

The priest replied, "Yes, The Western Ocean is between the shores of the New World where the thirteen colonies are located and Europe. West of Africa. Waters West of Europe. Hence, Western Ocean. The Eastern or Indian Ocean is where India dips into the waters...that body of water is on the other side of the New World...I have heard some refer to that as *Pacificum* or simply the Pacific."

"And what of it?" The nun asked.

The priest answered, "Captain Cook is charged with locating an ice-free navigable passage to the American Hudson Bay. The Admiralty is going to commission this voyage for twenty thousand pounds."

"Did he share that during his last confession with you, Father?" The nun asked with a playful smile.

"Oh, no, Sister. It came up when he mentioned there is a cargo ship in our ports which will soon be bound for the New World," the Priest explained.

The nun remarked, "To voyage on a cargo ship would be miserable indeed."

"Yes. The savages in the New World would benefit greatly from God's love," the priest observed.

"Do you mean God's word as spoken by an ordained priest of our order or of any denomination?" The sister asked.

"Of any Christian denomination," the priest replied. "Before he died back in 1708, Jacques Gravier created the Kaskaskia Indian-French dictionary for the Illinois mission. But, now that Great Britain has had the Canadian colony since '63, I don't see much spread of Catholicism. The Jesuits have tried."

"I'm sure," the nun replied, "that the wars have hurt the spread of God's Word."

"The natives may feel resentful," the priest started, "The Natchez tribe was fully exterminated. Then, when the French attacked, they lost to the Chickasaws in 1736. Father Lenat, a Jesuit, accompanied the army and perished with them, dying at the stake at the hands of the Indians. And since '61, the Jesuit order has been suppressed by the monarchies of Spain, France and England. They thought the Jesuit order was becoming too politically influential."

"Yes, Father," the sister replied. "I heard all those Jesuit missionaries were taken to New Orleans, charged as criminals and shipped to the French.... That New World is now allowing the savages to supplant the Trinity." She crossed herself.

"We need faithful souls to be brave enough to go to the New World and spread God's Word," the Priest agreed.

"If you speak of all Christian faiths," the nun replied, "Reverend Joseph Fish attempted to minister to the

Narragansett Indians for a decade before he left in 1774. He even wrote a letter to Sam Niles whom he accused of influencing the Indians to not hear him preach."

The Priest replied, "Then there is that Joseph Johnson fellow. I received a copy of a letter from Eleazar Wheelock about Mr. Johnson sent 15th January of this very year, 1776." the Priest shared.

"Oh?" The nun replied, "And what did the letter say?"

"Mr. Johnson is a Mohegan Indian in the Colony of Connecticut. He became a very fine, educated, preacher," the priest recalled.

"Ah," The nun started, "a convert turned preacher to share God's word with his own people in the devastated American Colonies. I wonder if he has art to sell to fund his mission work..." she added.

"Oh, I wouldn't think so," the priest

started. "You must be thinking of the Jesuit Art being sold by the director of art of the Imperial Gallery in Vienna, Austria." He paused as he thought, "Joseph de Rosa, was his name."

"Well, I always thought," the nun started, "that Holy art was intended for the Church to provide encouragement to the people. When Queen Maria Teresa and her son, Joseph the second, start buying Holy art..." She shook her head, "for their private collection... to keep it away from the people..." She threw her hands up.

"Yes," the priest replied, "It is a pity. She will probably buy several paintings. I heard she fancies *Anthony van Dyck's* Madonna and Child with *Sts. Rosalia,* Peter, and Paul..."

The nun replied, "It is a weakness to allow such treasures to be sold. We need to have representatives of the church make prudent choices. Choices which benefit the people, otherwise, the masses will think all Catholics are weak, hypocritical, corrupt and willing to sell Holy treasures for the right price..."

They were both quiet for a moment. They both gazed quietly at the graveyard. Mrs. Mulhoolin was still there.

"Sister?" The priest asked. "Yes, Father?" the nun replied.

"Perhaps you can share the need to have examples of faith... with Mrs. Mulhoolin, there?" the Priest asked hesitantly.

"She is still not Catholic, Father." The nun reminded, "I don't think she is that warrior soul to share God's Word in the New World..." as she looked at the priest dubiously.

"Yes," The priest agreed, "but...If we support her, she would think fondly of our order. We can promise to keep a candle burning in the name of her husband... and perhaps she could open doors for us in the future in the Colonies...after the wars have died down a bit...It is possible the Catholic faith would be embraced by those living in the New World." He paused, then added, "If she has been faithful to the memory of her departed husband, and she did what she could to give her daughter a better future, she has integrity and a faithful soul." He looked pleadingly at the nun, "Sister,....Just present it to her as a possible choice.."

"What choice?" the sister asked.

"We would like to invite her to join our small group of missionaries planning to go to the New World. I'm sure I can convince our sailor to help us find passage on that cargo ship heading to the Colonies. If she does decide to join our missionaries, Mrs. Mulhoolin will have constant support of prayer, finances, and companionship to provide for her needs." he added.

The nun thought, "I suppose, father, I could remind her of your homily today." She paused as she recited, "Philippines 4:7 shall instruct you which option shall give you   peace, which transcends all understanding. The Holy Spirit shall calm your heart when you make the right choice, even if it is a difficult choice..." She looked at him for approval. "Shall I say that to the widow Mulhoolin?"

"Yes, good idea...while it is still fresh from mass..." The priest encouraged as he gestured toward the preoccupied widow Mulhoolin. "I shall remain inside unseen while you speak with her," he added, "then you can come in and tell me what happened..."

The nun watched the priest go inside.

She turned around to look at the back of Mrs. Mulhoolin quietly looking down at the grave of her husband.

The sister took a deep breath, looked up into the sun, and then walked softly to the widow, and gingerly approached Mrs. Mulhoolin saying, "Good afternoon, Mrs. Mulhoolin. Nice to see you, again." She smiled, "Did I hear you humming a tune?"

The widow wiped a tear from her eye and turned around surprised to see the nun.

Mrs. Mulhoolin replied, "Yes. Yes," she explained, "I was humming ...from the *Beggar's Opera...*"

Then, Mrs. Mulhoolin sang the tune and softly spoke the words, "*O Waly, Waly up the bank. Farewell, farewell, all hope of bliss. For Polly always must be thine ...you should reward a constant heart since alas 'tis so seldom found...*" Mrs. Mulhoolin trailed off toward the end and smiled bashfully.

"Ah, yes, your daughter Polly is in the Colonies. Mrs. Mulhoolin..." the nun started again, "Have you considered?" "Considered what, Sister?" Mrs. Mulholin asked.

The nun replied, "Staying in Ireland..."

"Yes. I was born here, married here,

and intend to join my husband in death here in this verdant land."

The nun replied, "Yes. You can stay and pray for your Polly or leave and look for Polly..." The nun immediately regretted saying such a succinct and blunt statement.

She looked at Mrs. Mulhoolin and dared not say another word. They both stood there in silence.

Then, Mrs. Mulhoolin's throat tightened. She tried to steady her breath by breathing deeply, hoping to prevent the avalanche of tears from erupting. Breath in, then out. In, then out.

But, then Mrs. Mulhoolin succumbed...and sobbed, *"A stóirín, a leanbh ... Cronaim thu..."* Mrs. Mulhoolin's voice cracked.

The nun reached a hand out to hold the hand of Mrs. Mulhoolin.

Mrs. Mulhoolin struggled to find her

handkerchief as she covered her mouth to muffle her sobs. She choked when she tried to speak. She squeezed her eyes shut as she rushed to the nun, clinging tightly to her. The nun gasped for breath as she looked back to the church to see if the priest was watching from the window.

In her thoughts, Mrs. Mulhoolin repeated the words she had just spoken... *my dear, my child...I miss you...*

2 CHAPTER 31: (MARCH 1776)
Susanna Goes Shopping

In the center of Meeting Town, Susanna Wright walked amongst the open air carts. She stopped to speak with a merchant selling hand carved wooden lace bobbins. "I'll need four of those, please," Susanna said while proffering a coin.

The merchant selected four smooth curved lace bobbins about six inches long each, wrapped them in paper, and handed the bundle to Miss Susanna Wright. She placed the parcel in her basket.

The merchant then leaned over to her and whispered, "The lobster backs discovered our place. We need to have the gents meet somewhere new. Can you find it?"

Susanna loudly replied, "These are fine bobbins, but I also need a shuttle. What have you for my tatting?" She softly whispered to him, "I've already been looking for places which may have egress options."

He whispered back as he selected a small shuttle for tatting and presented it to her. "When you locate it, let me know so I may position my cart. I shall also need to alert the farmer so he can bring libations. Still need to ensure no Loyalists poison our water, eh?"

Then, a red coat wandered by looking at the sewing notions offered by this merchant.

Susanna Wright fingered the lace shuttle, then handed it back to the merchant, "Thank you, Sir. I will think about it, but won't purchase today."

Susanna wright looked at the Red Coat, "Good evening to you, Sir. Lovely weather, isn't it?"

"I'm new here, madame, but have heard small coastal towns might have isolated storms." he replied.

"Indeed? Well, our sailors must appreciate the smooth waters and fine weather, while they still can, then. We wouldn't want to see another four thousand souls perish as did in last September's Newfoundland's disaster."

"No, I'm sure even if it does storm, the skilled men here would not allow a single soul to drown, so it *shan't...shall not...* be in the newspapers as was that Newfoundland tempest of '75."

The solder smiled at Susanna Wright and bade her, "Good day," then he

21

turned to leave.

Susanna smiled at his departing form, glanced briefly at the merchant who was now approaching a new customer.

Then, making sure nobody was watching her or about to follow her, Susanna Wright walked quickly away.

3 CHAPTER 32: (MARCH 1776): Polly and Jane in the Carriage discuss Cosmetics

Still awaiting the return of Billy Dawes and Silversmith to finish butchering the wild boar which attacked Polly Mulhoolin, leaving her disheveled at the side of the road on which they had travelled, Polly and Jane continued to chat.

"My, my." Jane commented as she put

the brush away into her carpet bag. "Polly, that tale of how you came to this country is riveting. My own voyage with Silversmith was rough, but not like that."

Jane exhaled as she sat back against the cushioned seats inside the carriage.

The morning sunbeams caressed the earth, making the dewdrops on the tips of each grass blade sparkle into a carpet of diamonds. Jane opened the carriage door and inhaled the sweet air.

"I'd say your staff has been gone for a couple of hours, Miss Jane," Polly commented.

"That's to be expected," Jane replied, "butchering a beast in the wilderness... even with Silversmith's favorite knives, is bound to take a while. It gives us time to transform you into a more presentable version." Jane handed Polly a tiny mirror, which fit snugly into the palm of her hand.

Polly Mulhoolin, looked at her reflection in the small mirror Jane had proffered. She was indeed a much cleaner version than when the travelling party had found Polly on the side of the road a couple hours earlier.

"You look quite respectable, indeed, Polly," Jane nodded with approval.

"Do you think this Dunlaps family will provide lodging for me, then?" Polly asked while looking at her hair now neatly combed and tied into a bun. The blood had been washed off her face and Jane had loaned her a shawl to cover the blood and dirt on her dress. At least the bodice. Not much one could do to hide blood stains on Polly's skirts.

"All we can do is try," Jane encouraged, "Perhaps when Silversmith runs her errands, she can purchase fabric for a new skirt for you to make. May I assume you make your own clothes?" Jane asked.

"I do, yes. I'm quite adept with a needle and thread. I learned when I arrived, here." Polly admitted.

"Oh," Jane shared, "I think I see them returning henceforth. Once they get the butchered meat loaded, we can resume our travels, Polly."

"Could I make myself useful with the loading?" Polly asked as she moved to get out of the carriage. "I'm sure we can all help each other," Jane said as she opend the carriage door and hopped out.

Both Billy and Silversmith were smiling, "We'll need to make a couple more trips," Billy shared, "Miss Jane, I would mind your dress, Miss. Wouldn't want you to arrive at an estate with blood on your skirts."

"Oh, right." Jane remembered, "I'll remain inside the carriage".

"Well, I've already got blood on my skirts from that beast," Polly added.

"After we load," Bill said grunting while heaving part of the carcass up onto the perch where he would be seated while driving, "I'll take you ladies to the Dunlap residence. We can ask them to take this boar meat in exchange for Miss Polly's lodgings."

"But, we need to go to Lady Sarah Wilson's estate," Silversmith reminded.

"Aye," Billy started, "and I'll be sleeping in her ladyship's stable with my horses. Don't' want anything to happen to 'em. And, I could use fresh hay to lay my head on. We can go to the estate of Lady Sarah Wilson first to deposit your belongings. Unloading your personal travel items will provide more available space with which to better secure the pork meat. I could conduct the re-arrangement during the time you introduce yourself to Lady Wilson's household staff. After your introductions have been made, I should also have completed securing the meat, which would then permit me to drive the three of you to the Dunlap Printer's home."

27

"Do you need me to sit aside that carcass up there with you, Mr. Dawes, to make sure it don't fall off while you drive?" Silversmith offered.

Billy slowly turned to Silversmith. "It would be unusual for a passenger to ride atop with me, Miss Silversmith, but..."He blushed, "I would yearn for any excuse to have you at my side if you and your Mistress approves of such travel arrangements..." His voice trailed off as his gaze fixated on his own feet.

"I'm sure Miss Jane would allow it?" Silversmith asked turning to Jane.

Jane smiled from within the cabin of the carriage and, after the carcass was fully loaded, Billy helped Silversmith to ride atop next to him, with the excuse that somebody needed to mind the laundry bags containing the carcass of the pork.

The items were re-arranged, and then securely tied down. Billy Dawes wanted to ensure his plan was successful in order to possibly encourage a future opportunity to be close to Silversmith. If he could prove to Silversmith's Mistress, Miss Jane, that he was trustworthy and respectful, he would cement the trust needed with Silversmith's employer to nearly guarantee a future encounter.

Mr. Billy Dawes, having experienced many sorts of passengers as a carriage driver, discerned that the character of Silversmith was sincere, honest, and singularly rare. To himself, he noted that spending time next to Silversmith would be most agreeable indeed.

Inside the carriage rode Polly and Jane. Atop, next to Billie Dawes, sat Silversmith, who pulled a shawl around her head and shoulders as the breeze softly brushed against Silversmith's cheek. Billy looked over at Silversmith to ensure she was comfortable before he snapped the reins on the steeds.

Then, Billy and the three ladies, and one wild boar carcass resumed their travels.

4 CHAPTER 33: (APRIL 1776)
Questions of Bryce and Witherspoon.

Inside the Hargreaves residence, the butler Witherspoon looked around. His sleeves were rolled up as he finished polishing the silver.

It was so empty now, he thought as he put down a silver creamer. Miss Jane had been gone for nearly a month, now...

He had mended nearly everything that was on his list of projects to get to when he had time. Now that he did have time and was in this empty home, he longed for company.

Then, there was a knock on the door.

Witherspoon quickly jumped up, rolled down his sleeves, donned his jacket and opened the door briskly. Bryce Aiden Tyler, Jane's deceased Uncle Floyd's business partner, was about to wrap the door again with his fist just as Witherspoon yanked the heavy door opened.

"Witherspoon. Glad to see you home, my man." Mr. Tyler started. "Miss Jane has not yet returned, Sir." Witherspoon explained to him

"May I come in, Witherspoon?" Bryce asked as he combed back his hair with his fingers waiting to be invited into the Hargreaves residence, "This was after all my business partner's home, Witherspoon. If you have been in communication with Miss Hargreaves' maid, Silversmith, I would like to discover what they have learned. Does she still suspect her uncle was murdered?"

"Sir?" Witherspoon stepped aside while Bryce walked into the foyer.

Bryce Aiden Tyler took one step toward the library where he usually met with Jane's Uncle Floyd...but then paused with a lost expression. He knew he could not go to the room he would usually go to when Floyd Hargreaves was alive.

His clear green eyes looked at Witherspoon helplessly. He tugged on his freshly pressed waistcoat.

Not a formal foppish silky sort, but a simple one crafted of locally woven fabric.

Mr. Tyler preferred to buy from the local merchants instead of waiting for ships to arrive from Europe and the Far

East for the finer fabrics.

Despite the common fibers of his wardrobe, Bryce Aiden Tyler wore them as a man whose station was above that of the middling tradesman.

Bryce Aiden Tyler was a learned man from a family which had resided in the colonies for generations. This land was home for him. He did not yearn for Europe. His direct approach to business shocked Floyd Hargreaves when they first had met, but the two became fast friends, and then business partners, to grow a strong and successful trade.

"Would you please step toward the kitchen, Mr. Tyler?" Witherspoon offered to direct the silent and absolutely stationary Mr. Tyler "Are you here to discuss your occupation, Sir?"

Bryce Aide Tyler replied, "Witherspoon, every man in every occupation could imagine a better this or that..and one day the better 'this' would become a 'household that', provided that man diligently pursued his idea. "

"If I understand you correctly, Sir, you are saying that one must repeat the unfamiliar until it becomes familiar?" Witherspoon asked as he led the visitor down the hall.

"I have suspicions about Floyd Whiteney's death.," Bryce started now realizing how devastating to the business Uncle Floyd's death had been. He stopped walking as he continued, "Although I am endeavoring to embrace the overwhelming details of our joint venture without the aid of Mr.Hargreaves, I feel I must still devote energies toward finding out what really happened to my former business partner. For my own peace of mind. May we go into the library?"

"Sir?" Witherspoon arched one eyebrow.

Bryce Aiden Tyler walked toward the library where Jane's Uncle had died. He then turned to Witherspoon. "Miss Hargreaves is away investigating this invitation which her uncle received to attend an opera at some private estate."

"Sir?" Witherspoon commented, "Anybody who knew Mr. Hargreaves also knows he is not a supporter of the opera. He has other pastimes he prefers to pursue. Or...had pursued." Witherspoon followed Bryce down the hall to the library.

"You know how I value your opinion, Witherspoon. Tell me. Do you think Miss Hargreaves is correct? Did her Uncle Floyd, my business partner, do himself in? Or was he murdered?" Bryce challenged.

"Some of the townfolk, Sir," Witherspoon started, "believe it was a vengeful Indian spirit which took Mr. Hargreaves. Others say his cousin the inventor may have been jealous and done him in...Others, I dare say, think you are behind the plot to rid yourself of Mr. Hargreaves."

"I? They think it is I who did this dastardly thing to my friend and business partner?" Bryce protested, "Then, they do not know how difficult my life has become because I have no choice but to absorb the workload of Mr. Hargreaves, an impossible feat in and of itself. In addition to that, I also grieve over the loss of my friend." Bryce stood there with his hands on his hips, staring at Witherspoon. "What do you think, Witherspoon?"

Witherspoon paused a moment, looked down, then back up at Mr. Tyler. "Knowing your character after many years, I do not believe you caused Mr. Bryce to commit self murder," Witherspoon stated confidently as he stopped in front of the closed library doors. "But, I also do not believe you plotted his demise. You both relied on each other and you do not profit from his death."

"Then," Bryce Aiden Tyler replied as they stood in front of the the closed library, "Will you join me in a tiny informal investigation?"

"Sir?" Witherspoon asked.

Bryce Aiden Tyler explained, "Magistrate Pinkney says he is too busy trying to find out why his brother's lands were claimed and taken as property of the crown. Jane ...I mean Miss Hargreaves...has set out to find the truth about what happened to her uncle. So, I feel I must also do my part. I dare say I have not had sound sleep since the incident. I will only sleep soundly once I discover the facts of what led to the death of Floyd Hargreaves. So, will you help?"

Bryce flashed his winning smile.

"I shall endeavor to contribute to your efforts in any manner appropriate," Witherspoon commented.

"Then, let us start with your explanation regarding why the townsfolk believe an Indian spirit could have caused this." Bryce began, "I think we can dismiss the possibility that I did it. And I dare say his inventor cousin is far too busy to be concerned with doing it. So... the Indian spirit. Explain."

"The floor sir," Witherspoon indicated as he opened the door to the library, but did not step in. "I have not yet cleaned it, per Mistress Jane's orders. As you recall, you were both working on some sort of project and Mr. Hargreaves did not want any papers disturbed, so neither I nor Silversmith went in there to tidy...and the room got rather dusty. Mr. Hargreaves said he liked it that way."

"Hmmm," Bryce pondered, "but... he only used this library to be alone, yet I recall him favoring that chair over there." "In fact," he continued," I do not recollect one time when I have seen him at that desk where his body was found. Remember, Witherspoon. We would oft times take tea in the parlor and discuss business..." Bryce looked at the library floor without stepping inside, then added, "And there are ...no foot prints...no footprints?" Bryce's voice trailed off.

"Indeed, sir," Witherspoon started," Dust on the floor, yet no footprints in the dust...not even those of Mr. Hargreaves to get to the desk where he died."

Bryce muttered to himself, "No prints of a victim and no prints of an assailant."

Witherspoon continued, "Some say they heard a shot from over there, yet others said they heard a shot from over here when the town clock struck, and still others say they heard two shots after the clock struck the hour. With so many versions, it is as if the incident was fabricated..." The butler indicated with a troubled look.

"To add to that, sir," Witherspoon commented, "I know the cobbler who makes the shoes and the soles of Magistrate Pinkney and his brother and the doctor all came from the cobbler in town. He makes a unique pattern of the sole, but Mr. Hargreaves only wore shoes he purchased when he went on a business trip. This means that Mr. Hargreaves's shoe prints should be in the dust, but they are not."

Witherspoon stepped aside into the hallway and picked up a pair of shoes belonging to the former owner of the household. The pattern of the soles, he showed Mr. Tyler, was quite unique. A print of Mr. Hargreaves' shoes was nowhere to be seen on the dusty floor.

"I see," Bryce concurred, "So Mr. Floyd Hargreaves did not walk across the room to sit at the desk he never used. If he did shoot himself, he would have to have been standing over there...and then floated to the desk." Bryce looked at the ground, "I see the footprints of the doctor, Magistrate Pinkney and his brother. I see where they skidded while picking up the weight of the body... but I do not see the unique sole print of Floyd Hargreaves' shoes."

Witherspoon asked, "What would you like to do now, sir?"

Bryce thought a moment and said, "Magistrate Pinkney is occupied with erupting battles in the colonies, unrest with the natives of this land, and finding out why his brother's property was seized by the Crown. To convince him to formally investigate this, I think you and I need to present him with solid facts which prove this was murder." He smiled at Witherspoon, "Somebody went to considerable trouble to make murder look like self-murder. Shall we find out why?"

5 CHAPTER 34: (MARCH 1776) Polly and Jane Ride in the Carriage

As their carriage bumped along in the morning light, Jane continued speaking with Polly, "Polly, I can now understand why you have such suspicions of the British ...despite the fact that your own husband is from England. Not all people born in England hold to the opinions held by the monarchy. "

"I felt better when Silversmith told me she liked working for you, Miss Jane Hargreaves," Polly shared.

"Oh, Jane, please. Just call me Jane," Jane insisted, "You know, when I was living in England, before my parents died, we were wealthy enough to never have slaves. Every member of our house staff was paid for their work. My father believed putting his staff on a salary would encourage them to improve their skills instead. He said in the households with slaves, he noted resentment, laziness and even sabotage during daily duties."

"Then," Polly asked, "Did you bring your entire staff with you to this country?"

"When my fortunes changed," Jane explained, "and my inheritance was an allowance barely large enough to support myself and one servant and other fixed expenses. I...well, I gave all my servants an option to stay, assuming the man who inherited would keep them on. It turns out, he did not wish to employ any of my staff... So, before I made arrangements with Uncle Floyd to voyage over here, I was determined to either find a new source of income for myself in order to provide for their salaries.... or I would find each servant a household which would pay them fairly. "

"And what happened?"

"I found each servant a new household," Jane smiled, "one which would provide more than simply room and board, as is offered to slaves."

"So, how many servants accompanied you over here?" Polly asked.

"Well, one. Silversmith." Jane shared. "Butlers, under-butlers, footmen, upstairs maids, downstairs maids, cooks, gardeners, stable boys, drivers...all stayed in England. And the heir to my father's estate is enjoying the summer house, the house in London, all the homes... he's quite happy, I'm sure."

"Yes, it is difficult to adjust to a new life," Polly sympathized.

Jane continued, "My uncle Floyd paid for our passage, Silversmith and me. Although he is more of the middling classes, my Uncle Floyd, always paid his staff. He, like the other Hargreaves, never had slaves."

"Society almost demands one to collect as many slaves as possible...especially out here, to run the untamed acreages." Polly commented.

Jane sighed, "One must always think of how life would be if they were in that position. These days, fortunes changes rather suddenly...as you know... Some seem to enjoy gathering numbers of slaves to boast about at parties, yet these same people are unable to manage them. So, the spiral continues: they cannot manage them, the people become resentful and rebellious, and now the master must resort to the most horrific punishments to try and force slaves to obey."

"Intelligent people don't work like that. They respond to respect," Polly abruptly shared. "Well, the problem is," Jane started, "that it is all legal. Cruel, but legal."

"Immoral, but legal," Polly added.

Jane commented, "Think of this. If nobody were allowed to have slaves. If nobody were permitted to mistreat nor kill slaves, it would force the masters to invent a more efficient way of working." Jane added, "These colonies need more inventors."

"There is no excuse for mistreating staff," Polly added sharply.

Jane whispered while crinkling her nose, "Let us discuss something a bit more frivolous." Jane smiled. "I believe we were talking about lip rouge. You started by telling me that you couldn't wear the color because you were married?"

Polly explained, "If Button and I had married in England, some would have invalidated my marriage if they had seen "me wear lip rouge. They would assume I didn't love my husband and no longer wanted to be married."

"But," Jane protested, "white faces and red lips are what all the ladies in court wear. It is the fashion of those born into power and wealth. Red lips are not an indicator of fidelity."

"Before I earned my freedom and fulfilled my contract," Polly started, "I met people in town who were very firm on the matter: No lip color."

Jane replied, "Oh, you mean those Puritans. They make such a fuss over the smallest things. Lip color. Imagine." Jane shrugged as she applied the stain to her own lips, "I have never married and I have no problem showing my class by wearing it."

Jane looked at Polly with wide eyes, "Are you aware, Polly, Queen Elizabeth...the one who lived some two hundred years ago, wore lip color? I'll even wager Queen Charlotte wears it today." Jane emphatically rubbed her red lips together and smiled.

"Didn't British Parliament ban lip color?" Polly asked, "I'm not in touch with the politics of today."

"Oh," Jane agreed, " I am also not one for politics. There are no issues, which I care about. I feel politics is just some game that men play." Jane wrinkled her nose.

"Politics lead to rules of the land, Jane," Polly corrected. "All the people who live in the land, are governed by the rules of that land."

Jane looked up, "Well, I'm sure some man tried to outlaw lip rouge. No doubt jealous of his wife and her *accouterments*. Lip color, I've heard, changes the balance of power between men and women."

Polly looked perplexed, "Pardon?'

Jane cleared her throat, "...something along the lines that men feel a woman will suddenly become powerful enough to hypnotically seduce men into matrimony by cosmetic means"

Polly blurted out, "That is nonsense."

Jane continued, "Apparently red lips renders men helpless. I suppose they have no will of their own whatsoever." Jane shrugged. "In France, nearly all the aristocracy wear *paint: blanc* and rouge are worn by both men and women, you know. Besides, a powdered face and red lips reminds me to behave with a regal manner no matter what country I am in." Jane smiled as she popped her tiny lip pot container back in her bag.

"But, in France, they are extreme in the use of cosmetics." Polly added, "From what I had heard, that is."

"Well, there are times I choose a more natural look for myself." Suddenly Jane remembered, "That socialite, Kitty Fisher was a quite the beauty, but who wants to die at age twenty-three from lead poisoning?"

"I remember that story." Polly recollected, "That was nine years ago, back in 1767...when I was still in Ireland...before I got to England and then took the ship over here."

"I recall that poem *Ruide Headland* said something about the men and women of County Ulster. North of Ireland, isn't it? Is it not said that the people of that part of Ireland pride themselves on valor, boasting and strife?"

"I think," Polly started, "you mean the part which states: the men of Ulster are the fiercest warriors of all Ireland, and the queens and goddesses of Ulster are associated with battle and death..."

"But what I mean to say is if you are so fierce by legend, then why didn't one of your Irish women ever get bold enough to don cosmetics in Ireland?" Jane asked.

Polly replied, "I cannot speak for each citizen in County Ulster. Only for the house my mother ran. I never wore face paint no matter how popular it was. I do remember Kitty Fisher died from the opaque white paint she painted on her shoulders, neck and face. It was very popular and the people who manufactured the face paint never warned their customers of the dangers."

Jane frowned, "But are not people who make things only obligated to sell and see a profit? They are not obliged to warn the customer of the horrors contained within the product. That is why it is the manner of travelling sellers of goods to make absurd exaggerations about the benefits of their wares."

Polly replied, "But if it is fashion, then in essence it is killing everybody who succumbs to frivolity."

Jane defended, "I am quite aware one

should use cosmetics with caution. I myself use...or used to use the sheer paints made from vinegar or bismuth or even arsenic, which gives you that bright glow on your face. Perfectly safe ingredients."

"Don't gardeners use arsenic to kill rodents?" Polly asked.

"Oh, you'd have to ask Silversmith about that," Jane dismissed. "She learned gardening and such. I haven't the foggiest what they use. There are some things a lady should never get involved in. One is politics. And the other is ingredients, which might be used both on ones face...and perhaps in the elimination of rodents. Best to enjoy the bliss of ignorance."

Polly took a deep breath and observed, "I don't believe you really hold to that, Jane. Pardon my directness. Do you adopt a *façade* of *naïveté* to fit into your social circle? You strike me as one wanting facts, not ignorance."

"Well," Jane sighed, "That is a direct and forthright challenge, but I attribute that to your Irish-ness." Jane had struggled for the proper word and instead used her hand to grasp at the air for the appropriate term.

"Why might you harbor such apprehension?" Polly asked.

Jane took a deep breath, "Understand, Polly, I'm living in more humble accommodations than those in which I was raised. My sponsor, my uncle, who brought Silversmith and me over here, has recently died... I think we are all trying to find a way to ease into any social circle which will have us. I do not feel it my duty to right every wrong in the world. That is an exhausting burden I do not need."

Polly nodded and changed the subject. "I see. I apologize if I said something to..."

Polly looked at her hands unable to complete her sentence, then suddenly looked directly at Jane, indicating she had nothing left to say and was genuinely apologetic for offending her kind and benevolent new friend.

Jane shook her head, "No need for apologies. Let us forget all about it and be friends, shall we?"

"I feel an affinity for Silversmith as a fellow countryman. She has confidence in you, and I also will place my confidence in you, Miss Hargreaves," Polly explained.

"Thank you," Jane replied simply, "and do address me as 'Jane'. Think of me as a fellow sister who is trying to understand how to live in these untamed Colonies…"

"And do call me 'Polly'," Polly smiled shyly, "your devoted friend…or… sister whilst we both reside in this wild new land… perhaps one day, it shall prove to be an environment of opportunity."

6 CHAPTER 35: (APRIL 1776) Polly and Jane continue to chat

Jane glanced out the window of the carriage. They were passing trees and wild grasses. She adjusted her skirts as her legs were getting tingly from sitting in the same position. As Jane watched the passing scenery, she tried to see the driver. From her vantage point, she could not see anything other than the dust kicked up by horses galloping.

She turned to Polly and smiled.

Polly smiled back. She commented softly, "Your kindness rescued me and my unborn from certain death. Thank you."

Jane simply shook her head as if to indicate no thanks was needed, and added, "I'm sure you'd do the same for me if our situations were reversed."

"You being from England and me from Ireland... If I knew that, I honestly don't think I would, Jane."

"I see," Jane smiled politely.

"But,"Polly added, "seeing your manner is so contrary to the English I have encountered... Seeing how Silversmith puts her faith in you... After getting to know you, I would say if our situations were reversed, I would surely render aid as you have rendered to me today."

"Thank you, Polly. That is quite an endorsement. I'm sure we shall be grand friends," Jane smiled politely and resumed looking out the window.

There was a pause. A silent pause. A long pause.

Polly took a deep breath. " So, face powder... Can you get the sort you need over here in the colonies? The type you got back in Europe?" Polly asked.

"No, actually, " Jane explained pleased Polly decided to leave her vitriol behind. "I have not had time to explore all the boutiques here, but I do not think one can easily get what one is used to in London. What I can purchase is powdered clay or Bentonite."

"Bentonite?" Polly asked, "You mean what the furniture makers use to fill hallow legs to make the chair feel heavier and more sturdy?"

"Oh, no. That must be something else," Jane dismissed. "Benonite is what Pliney the Elder and even Cleopatra had used to tighten the skin. When mixed with vinegar, it makes a foamy poultice clay for the face, which deep cleans it once it dries until it cracks on your face. If you use just the dry powder, it will keep your face from shine all day."

"Isn't Bentonite green?" Polly asked.

"Well," Jane thought, "It does have a green-grey cast to it, but the color counteracts the ruddy tones in my face and the powder keeps my skin from being shiny. My skin was always shiny with the lead based *blancs*."

"So you found a face powder you like over here?" Polly asked, glad to speak of something inconsequential.

"But, I simply cannot relinquish the use of lip paint," Jane explained. "If I have to find cherries, or pomegranate seeds to stain my lips, I shall. I have heard of some who will scrape the white cochineal bugs from a cactus pad in the hotter climates and dry them, then grind them to use for the deep red color and mix with a touch of oil to apply to ones lips."

"Do you do that? Make your own?"

Polly asked.

Jane held up her hand in protest, "Oh, no. I purchase. I don't make. All I know is that when one has a bad day, a bit of red stain on one's lips makes one feel as if they are in the French Courts, you see."

Polly commented, "I suppose cosmetic paints might have a different meaning in this country."

"Last I checked," Jane started with a smile, "...we don't have any Queens nor Kings on this island to cause a silly fuss about which cosmetics and perfumes we can and cannot wear. We are all too busy trying to survive, you see."

"Yes. I can live without a ruling family quite easily," Pollyagreed. "I learned a couple of languages as a child, so have seen the impact kings and queens have on people of different cultures."

"Different languages?" Jane asked.

"English, German, French... some Italian and a touch of Latin," Polly replied.

"To have studied all those languages, you must also have fine penmanship."

"I believe I do," Polly replied.

"A shame your talents were wasted as a housemaid," said Jane. "I now look for opportunities to give to Silversmith to expand her talents. A challenge makes one grow, don't you think? I do hope Silversmith does not feel trapped in her current position..." Suddenly, Jane sat up straight with the practiced motion reminiscent of a lady snapping an open fan shut to make a point without stating a word. Then Jane continued, "I've made up my mind, Polly. You have inspired me. I shall look for ways to challenge Silversmith..." Jane smiled brightly.

"I'm glad. I may not know Silversmith personally, but I do know the Irish spirit is strong and ready for a challenge," Polly observed.

Jane extracted a bore-bristle hairbrush and looked at it. "I know their hair was stiff enough to make a good brush, but I never really thought much about how one may taste. Boiled, roasted or fried..." She smiled at Polly, "You've given me a different perspective on several things to which I had not previously given much thought."

"And you," whispered Polly, "are helping me to find lodgings so perhaps I can find out if my husband lives or has been scalped or enslaved..."

"I think you are presentable enough to convince the Dunlap printers to take you in. You'll have to write to me and tell me how you fare," Jane smiled.

"Write to you?" Polly asked, "So, you won't be staying in the area? You won't visit me when the baby arrives, then?"

"I know it looks as if I've packed for an extended venture, but I'll only be staying a couple of days. Then return home to determine where Silversmith and I shall live next..." Jane's voice trailed off. "I always prepare for the absolute worst case...but I'd like to make sure you are situated properly. It is only fitting. We can write to each other. A Quill with a bit of ink and warmed sealing wax could convey a message of friendship and comfort to wherever, in this vast wilderness, your log-structure is located."

Polly took a deep breath as she gazed out her own window. "I don't think I can ever go back to our log home. Button and I had a dream of building twenty or thirty homes ...owning hundreds of acres... That's now a shattered dream...." Polly trailed off.

"Nonsense," Jane encouraged, "Just modify your dream to build twenty-nine...thirty is far too ostentatious, but twenty-nine is a more lady-like goal...even if you must collect the materials and build them all by yourself, focus on that goal. God would not inspire your dream if God does not provide the tools with which you may obtain that goal." Jane smiled realizing that perhaps that was more of a reminder to herself to maintain hope for justice as much as a warm encouragement to Polly.

Polly held a palm up to hide her smile at the image which had just manifested in her mind. "I'd have to dress in trousers, get the papers of ownership, and then dress like a man when I obtain supplies..." Polly chortled at the absurd concept of herself wearing trousers like a man so she could build a cabin in the woods.

"Then you must dress in trousers to obtain your home building supplies and wear lip rouge to have fun...maybe even wear them both at the same time," Jane chuckled, "If building is your dream. Do it. Don't blame circumstances to stop you from achieving... there will always be something to blame until you decide to stop blaming, and start taking a purposeful step toward your future."

"Future?" Polly shook her head as if

she pictured a rather bleak tomorrow.

Jane continued, "Yes... a future of hard work, but also of great rewards reaped by your future generations." Jane smiled at Polly's belly, then back up to Polly's face, Jane clearly stated, "Now, back to concentrating on today. Let us see if the Dunlaps enjoy Silversmith's unusual concept of fried pig belly for a morning snack..."

"And what if these Dunlaps don't take me in, Jane? What if wild boar meat or this fried Bacoun... is not accepted as my lodging fee?" Polly asked.

7 CHAPTER 36: (MARCH 1776)
Silversmith at the Wilson Mansion

Silversmith was stumbling under the weight of the bags. She squeezed through the servants entrance to find the kitchen was crowded with staff.

"Is this area called Rising Sun?" Silversmith asked a woman who looked like a housekeeper.

That woman, one of Lady Sarah Wilson's housekeepers, beckoned Silversmith to follow in order to show Silversmith to Jane Hargreaves' room, where Silversmith dropped off some of the bags.

"Yes," the housekeeper replied.

"If I need to run errands, are there shops nearby this estate?"

"No," the housekeeper answered, "Summer Hill is small, but remote."

"Am I in Summer Hill or Rising Sun?" Silversmith asked confused.

The housekeeper replied, "William Penn and his Quakers settled the area in 1702, calling it Summer Hill. In 1720, Henry Reynolds built a tavern and coach stop. He had a sign with a picture of a sun rising over the horizon, so some call this place Rising Sun."

"Coach?" Silversmith asked, "As in horses for hire?"

"You and your mistress may wish to know Nottingham Lot seventeen is the only place to hire a horse if you need to run errands."

"How far is it from here? A walk?" Silversmith asked, "How far do the horses go?".

The housekeeper replied, "Nottingham Lot seventeen is a long and healthy walk from here, but their hired horses will take you anywhere you wish. "

Then, after most of the luggage was deposited in the room where Jane would stay, Silversmith was left with just one simple bag. The housekeeper took Silversmith upstairs to where she would be staying. She was instructed on the proper staircase to ascend and descend to attend to her mistress' needs.

The housekeeper explained, "Each of the master rooms has several hooks which trigger a bell in each one of the servants quarters. So, each guest room has two pull cords. One for the main servants' hall and one, to use at night, to a specific servant. The room where your employer will stay is connected to the room upstairs where you will stay."

"So only I will be awakened by my employer?" Silversmith asked.

"Correct," said the housekeeper as she pointed to a bell in the corner of the room where Silversmith was to sleep. The room was the size of a large closet. The bed was small and narrow, pushed up against the wall. The only furnishings were one table with one drawer, a single candle in its candle stick, and a chamber pot in the far corner.

The housekeeper continued, "And we don't rename you after your master's name, so you will always be named your name. Since the guests invited have been asked to remain for the season, we placed a wooden plank on your door and there is a paint brush and can there. Select a symbol and that is how you will be known," the housekeeper pointed to some of the other rooms which had a square, circle, etc..

"Could I simply write my name?" Silversmith asked.

The housekeeper stopped and gave a single sharp laugh, "You write?" Then when Silversmith didn't respond in kind, the housekeeper added, "You can do what you like. Just remember, if you do write, not everybody reads. We need to know what room you'll be in. You may leave suddenly or stay the whole of summer. We don't know..."

The housekeeper walked down the hall and opened a cupboard. "Linens here," she said.

"Oh, that's very forward thinking," Silversmith commented, trying to put Lady Sarah Wilson's housekeeper at ease.

The housekeeper handed Silversmith some folded sheets for her to make up her own bed. "I'll leave you to unpack then." The housekeeper started for the door.

Silversmith hurried after her, with folded sheets still in hand. "Ma'am? I've been asked to run an errand. So, I won't have time to unpack now as I must leave immediately." Silversmith ran back to her room, and dropped her bag on the mattress along with the folded sheets. The housekeeper was already walking away. Silversmith hurried after her down the hallway.

As Silversmith bustled after the housekeeper, she called, "I would so appreciate any insight on the background of the other guests, if you could share that," Silversmith urged.

"You've never been here, then. I don't recall you." The housekeeper grunted.

"No Ma'am. This is my first time at the estate," Silversmith commented.

"The basics, then. Follow me as I've plenty to do. The lady of the house is Miss Sarah Wilson... from Carolina society." The housekeeper hurried off assuming Silversmith was keeping up.

"I've not been to the Colony of Carolina," Silversmith responded.

The housekeeper shared, "I've been with her... Lady Sarah Wilson... since she arrived in this country. Well, since she ran away and gained position in society."

"Ran away?" Silversmith commented.

"Lady Sarah Wilson, that's your hostess' name, is very open about her history," the housekeeper started. "She says that prevents blackmailers from trying to elicit money from her. So she's quite public about her background."

"Background?" Silversmith echoed.

The housekeeper bustled past the other staff in the hallway as she headed back downstairs. "Sarah Wilson, part of Queen Charlotte's court, eloped in 1771 with a diamond necklace...not a man. She was caught and shipped to the American colonies to be sold as a slave here, but she ran away right after she was purchased. She changed her name to *Marchioness de Waldegrave,* Sister of the Queen. After all, she had stolen a few trinkets from Queen Charlotte that would make her story believable. She consorted with Carolina society for over a year. Those society doors opened along with their purses, all fawning to impress the queen's sister."

"But if she wasn't the queen's sister, wasn't her story a lie?" Silversmith asked.

"That was her income. She was a confidence trickster. It was her occupation. But she always paid her loyal staff, so who am I to judge where her money comes from as long as I get paid?" The housekeeper shrugged as she burst through the busy kitchen where the staff was already chopping and slicing.

The housekeeper continued, "Eventually, the truth caught up with *Marchioness de Waldegrave,* and she changed her name back to Sarah Wilson and acquired this estate, promising never to return to either Carolina colony. In today's modern times of 1776 she spends her efforts entertaining in hopes of finding a legitimate heir of some sort to marry."

"I see," Said Silversmith astonished. "She was never arrested?"

"Indeed not. They couldn't find enough evidence, so she has no record. She was savvy enough to have befriended influential authorities of the area so they took pity on her and simply asked her to leave, which we were already preparing to do. It doesn't matter to me. A house needs running no matter where it is."

"So how should I address the mistress of this estate? Lady Sarah Wilson? Marchioness de Waldegrave? or Miss Sarah? "

"If you want to be on her good side, I'd pick either Lady or Duchess Wilson. She thinks if you say a title frequently enough, it'll stick. This home is called the Wilson estate. It's not named something memorable like... Evenfalls. The lands are slight. We only have this structure and the stable out back with a space for the stable boys to sleep in."

"So, she collected enough money to purchase it?" Silversmith prodded.

"Well, no. She's had numerous paramours whose gifts provided for this estate. She doesn't own this land, but you must always act as if she does or she'll throw you out. Her ladyship has no tolerance for people who attempt to demean her standing in society."

"Noted. Thank you. Where is the owner of this estate?" Silversmith asked.

"The owner is in Europe." The housekeeper shrugged.

"Ah," Silversmith said, "And what of the other guests? Are they of society? I don't want to offend them, you see...this being my first time here...at the Wilson Estate?"

"Those invited or those who will actually come? Let's see, Abigail *Stoneman*. Owner of the Merchant's Coffee House and Tea House... and she's talking about opening up a ballroom in Newport...she was invited."

"Didn't she have a coffee house in Boston... at the site of the March '70 Massacre?"

"She did, but her family perseveres. Let's see... another Bostonian is arriving. Elizabeth Hager. She re- shoes horses."

"Blacksmith Handy Betty?"

"That's the one! She's bringing her friend from Maryland, Jane Burgess, also a blacksmith, called widow blacksmith as of 1773. She runs her husband's business now." The housekeeper replied.

"So the guest list is not actual society, but rather trades folk? Blacksmiths?" Silversmith prodded.

The housekeeper thought, "I think the Butterworth twins will be coming, but their mother won't, rest her soul. Mary Peck Butterworth was nearly 90 when she died last year, 1775. It was a February funeral. Lady Wilson was most upset, but she still plans to invite the twin boys, in their 40's now...Lady Sarah Wilson doesn't want to chance being lonely, you see..."

"Is the Butterworth family in a trade, as well?" Silversmith asked.

"Of sorts," the housekeeper explained. "Mary Butterworth was a Puritan housewife who became wealthy from counterfeiting over 1,000 pounds of currency and teaching others to join her enterprise. Never got convicted."

"Never?" Silversmith asked.

The housekeeper shrugged, "She came from a prominent family, so the townsfolk looked the other way. She may have spent a few days in jail, but never formally convicted. "

"So just her family name kept her from prison?" Silversmith asked.

"How did they put it...," The housekeeper thought a moment as she recollected, "...vehemently suspected to be guilty of making counterfeiting and uttering the bills of public credit in New England, particularly the Bills of his Majesty's Province of Massachusetts Bay and the Colony of Road Island, I think it was. Lady Sarah Wilson respected Mary Butterworth. She was inventive."

"Inventive? With copying pound notes?" Silversmith asked.

"She was a housekeeping artist," the housekeeper explained with a smile of admiration. "She would take starched cotton cloth, iron a genuine bill to lift the ink, then iron that onto a blank paper and touch up the artwork with her quill pen. She'd sell her bills off at half the face value of the bill."

"So, does Lady Sarah Wilson prefer to invite mostly women to her *soirées*?"

Silversmith asked.

The entire kitchen staff were busy organizing provisions in anticipation of several guests arriving all at once.

"Well, the men are all business sorts," the housekeeper explained. "When they decide to make an appearance... I don't know how they make money, but they always seem to have plenty of it. They are frequent guests here. But the women... the learned ones... all seem to be friends of Benjamin Franklin, and for some reason Lady Wilson keeps inviting them, but they politely decline, then later get together to meet in that town about one day's carriage ride away."

"Why do they meet there instead of coming here?" Silversmith asked as she stepped out of the way of the pantry being restocked with dry goods from other members of the household.

"I don't rightly know," The housekeeper shared,

"Maybe they prefer catching a glimpse of Benjamin Franklin instead of having a proper meal, here. And I don't rightly care, neither. Fewer guests means less work for me..." The housekeeper replied.

"Agreed." Silversmith said, "So, does Lady Wilson have friends from the Carolina Colonies?"

The housekeeper thought as she handed Silversmith some sacks of flour to hold while she reached behind them in the pantry to get a spare iron. "Lady Wilson may have met the Timothy family when she was in South Carolina. Peter Timothy had a sweetheart and I think Sarah Wilson wanted to seduce the man away."

"Seduce?" Silversmith repeated.

"Well, that Peter Timothy's mother, Elizabeth Timothy, was a widow who ran the South Carolina Gazette. Smart business woman. She knew how to make money and Lady Sarah Wilson was always friendly to those who could supply her with money."

The housekeeper sniffed as she walked to the hearth, stoked the fire, then placed the iron on the hot embers. She looked at a stack of washed, wrinkled cloth napkins.

"Tell me more about Elizabeth Timothy," Silversmith prodded.

The housekeeper accidentally knocked over a portion of the linen napkins. She retrieved some of the napkins from the floor, and then walked to the table to fold them.

"I'd have one of the girls do this folding, but they are all scrambling to prepare the house for guests, you see..." The Housekeeper commented.

The housekeeper folded a napkin, and picked up the next one, glancing at the iron in the hearth to see if it was hot enough. "Elizabeth Timothy was with child when her husband Lewis Timothy died back in 1739. Fell off a horse, I think. She printed an announcement that even though she's expecting her seventh child, she'd still run the paper. So her son, Peter, would be nearly 40 years old by today."

"And how did the South Carolina Gazette fare being run by a mother of seven children?" Silversmith asked.

"The business prospered," the housekeeper replied glancing at the fireplace to see if the iron was hot, yet. She continued, "Even started to sell pocket Bibles and other books about courtship and marriage around 1746."

"So, does this Elizabeth or Peter Timothy, do they meet in town with the ambassador Benjamin Franklin or do they come here to the estate?" Silversmith asked.

"The Timothy family has never been here," The housekeeper stated. "I'd say they would meet with Mr. Franklin if he were passing through the Meeting Town. They say that Mr. Franklin invested in

Mrs.Timothy's South Carolina Gazette. Supposedly, her Dutch work manner coupled with Mr. Benjamin Franklin's investment gold, helped the widow Timothy be the first woman newspaperman in South Carolina. So, it is natural to assume that Mr. Franklin would welcome any of the Timothy family when Mr. Franklin is in Meeting town."

"Meeting town?" Silversmith asked.

"Well, Meeting Town is the local name for it. It is a full day's carriage ride away. That's where the respectable folk go and meet. Timothy, Wright, and...."

"Wright?" Silversmith asked.

"Susanna Wright. She is acquainted with Mr. Franklin, as well... Don't tell me you've never heard of Susanna Wright"

"I don't think I have," Silversmith confessed.

"I dare say..." The housekeeper shook her head. She strode to the hearth and licked her finger, then tapped the handle of the iron. Now satisfied it was hot enough, she grabbed a dry rag, wrapped it around her hand, like a make-shift glove, and picked up the handle of the iron, returning to the table piled with linen napkins.

Silversmith said, "Well, I have heard of Benjamin Franklin. He's the ambassador to England."

The housekeeper took some un-ironed linens and laid them on the table before her. She dipped her free hand into a bucket of water, sitting nearby and sprinkled the linen napkin with water from her fingers, then she ironed it and handed it to Silversmith to fold.

The housekeeper responded to Silversmith with, "Indeed, he is. Benjamin Franklin took one of Miss Wright's dyed silk bolts over to Queen Charlotte as a gift. A diplomatic gift. Something about showing the Queen how the Colonies can make quality goods."

"So Susanna Wright is a silk worm farmer or some type of fabric weaver?" Silversmith queried as she folded the napkins. The housekeeper was quickly flicking water on the squares of cloth, swiping each one with the heat of the iron and pushing it to Silversmith, then grabbing the next one. Silversmith was trying to keep up with the pace.

"Miss Wright was first in her Pennsylvania colony to export silks. She has never married because, as a Quaker, she felt once she married, she would have to be subservient to men. But as a single business woman, she could conduct business as an equal with the men. Not only could she conduct business with them, they would respect her as an equal."

"So the two friends of Benjamin Franklin, the older ladies, Elizabeth Timothy, the newspaper publisher and Susanna Wright, the Quaker silk farmer, will be in this Meeting town instead of coming here to the estate of Lady Sarah Wilson?" Silversmith clarified.

"Well, Elizabeth Timothy might have died, but one of her seven children should be around. She wrote some books, you see... so the children stock them in the bookstores in town."

"Oh, speaking of selling things in town," Silversmith rose from the table, having folded the last napkin, "I have been instructed to purchase some items in town and I believe the carriage is waiting outside. Is there anything else I could help with before I run the errands, then come back and unpack?"

"Nay. Be off with you to run your errand. If you help in the household, then you are welcomed to stay for the season... you are called 'Silversmith'?" The housekeeper asked.

Silversmith smiled and turned to leave through the kitchen door. The carriage was waiting for her, Billy Dawes sitting on top with reins in hand. Jane had stepped out onto the gravel driveway.

"Oh, there is my mistress, now," Silversmith said, "Thank you so much," she said to the housekeeper.

The housekeeper went to a chalkboard on the wall and looked at the names. Her finger stopped at Hargreaves.

"Oi!" the housekeeper shouted at Silversmith, who turned around just outside the kitchen door. The housekeeper bustled after her.

"Mistress?" The housekeeper challenged, "my board says Master Hargreaves." The housekeeper looked skeptically at Silversmith. "The invitation was sent and accepted by a Mister...not a Miss. Not a Missus. Not a Dame....." she put her hands on her hips as she approached Silversmith, "What goes on, here? We demand honesty and integrity in this household. Explain yourself."

"Yes. Well..." Silversmith haltingly started, awkwardly looking at her Mistress Jane, "Mistress Jane is here representing her Uncle Floyd, so really the only adjustment to make is to note that Miss Jane will NOT be able to address the loneliness of Lady Sarah Wilson quite the way Lady Wilson may have originally uh...anticipated." She laughed nervously while thinking of what else to say to calm the territorial housekeeper.

Silversmith added, "If I may take the liberty, I find you very knowledgeable and feel I would learn so much from you during my stay. I... I think Miss Hargreaves will find... the company of the other guests...also...invigorating."

With that the housekeeper relaxed and said, "Aye. Always good to be around folk who share your judgements. Tend to your mistress, then... I just think Lady Sarah Wilson would have preferred a Floyd over a Jane..."

The housekeeper shrugged, again, walked back into the kitchen to correct the names on the chalk board. Another kitchen staff member closed the door behind the housekeeper.

Silversmith walked quickly to the carriage.

8 CHAPTER 37: (APRIL 1776) Bryce and Witherspoon Identify Possibilities

Inside the Hargreaves residence, both the Hargreaves' butler, Witherspoon, and Bryce Aiden Tyler, the business partner of the deceased, continued their informal investigation of Floyd Hargreaves's death.

They were both doubtful that it was "self-murder", as Magistrate Pinkney was quick to assess, however neither were they able to ascertain how it could have been executed, if it were murder.

89

These two men struggled in their efforts to create a plausible explanation satisfactory enough to gain the attention of Magistrate Karl Pinkney to actually open a formal investigation and capture the culprit.

Mr. Tyler paced as he and the Hargreaves' butler discussed possibilities of how this unfortunate circumstance could have been performed by one of devious intentions.

"If the shot came from where those standing outside heard the shot, then how could it have hit Mr. Hargreaves if he was over there?" Bryce took two strides and stopped as he a bit his lip and thought, "The angle is incorrect."

"Sir, may I be so bold as to inquire..." Witherspoon started while clearing his throat.

Bryce replied, "If you are to help me unravel this mystery, then I invite you to actively participate in this conversation. Witherspoon, I am eager to find who –not which tribal spirit- purposed to enact this foul deed. Ask."

"Sir, what, if I may, inquire... what was the nature of the argument you had with Mr. Hargreaves?"

"Ah yes," Bryce replied. "Well, this is highly irregular for me to share this with you prior to speaking with Miss Hargreaves, but she is away indefinitely. Yes. Well. How shall I sum it up? I believe I require your assistance and perhaps if you knew the truth it would warrant your trust in me."

Bryce cleared his throat, "To begin... Floyd Hargreaves, my business partner, was approached by a man... an Indian fellow... fluent in English. Rather fluent. He said he knew there were businesses in the colonies who would hire some

91

Indians to take people and enslave them. He wanted to know if we were one of those businesses. His concern was that middling trades folk, such as we, were portraying the natives in a manner such as to encourage fear amongst the colonists. He felt the reputation of all tribes was being besmirched."

"Sir, I still do not understand why such a conversation would cause a disagreement between you and Mr. Hargreaves..." Witherspoon commented.

Bryce replied ashamed, "Mr. Hargreaves wanted to dedicate our resources to help fight such a scheme. I felt it was pointless... a distraction... a waste. We barely had enough staff to handle our business as it was... and this Indian affair was no concern of ours. We do not promote nor sell slaves, so why waste time on it? Mr. Hargreaves, however, felt that if we did not actively stop those organizing this endeavor, that it would eventually harm our business. He said it was my God given duty to ferret out the malfeasance and the malfeasant himself and hand him over to those in charge... to Magistrate Pinkney, as it were."

"And do you think the Magistrate would have dedicated his men to that investigation?" Witherspoon asked.

"In my considered opinion," Bryce started, "if Magistrate Pinkney believes investigating Floyd Hargreaves's death is pointless, he would not care about some educated Indian fellow who holds that the reputation of all tribes are being tainted by such activities." Bryce sighed, "I wanted to concentrate on our own business and let the slave traders attend to theirs. Mr. Hargreaves disagreed and felt that profit could be made if all businesses of all industry agreed to not use slave labor. This is why we argued."

"Do you, sir, employ slaves?" Witherspoon asked.

"Oh, everybody has slaves," Bryce defended. "Well, no more than necessary. I mean in my household... They are not as skilled as you are, Witherspoon. You could replace ten of them." Bryce looked down at the ground. "Yes. I see Mr. Hargreaves' point, now. How productive is it really when your staff is forced to do a task?" Bryce concluded.

Witherspoon replied, "I have always been paid well for my work. Mr. Hargreaves provided education when needed. Some in my profession seek out apprenticeships to pass on skills to the next generation." Witherspoon continued, "I doubt slaves are given such consideration."

Bryce pleaded, "I wish you would not take Mr. Hargreaves side on this one, Witherspoon. You see if some businesses employ slaves, they can place their product on the market for far cheaper. How can we compete with that?"

"By making a better product, Sir," Witherspoon replied, "Products manufactured by resistant hands and hearts of resentful saboteurs will always be inferior to those made by willing skilled workers."

"I see your point, now, Witherspoon." Bryce sighed, "If it was an inconsequential matter as I had originally thought, then... then... my business partner would not have been killed...."

"When I served as footman in another household, sir," Witherspoon shared as he adjusted his shirt cuff, "I was loaned to help at a *soirée* of the Widow Degraffenreidt and the Widow Stagg."

"How long ago?" Bryce asked.

"Some thirty years ago," Witherspoon continued. "During these and other events hosted by these women, they would give away slaves as door prizes."

"Really!" Bryce replied astounded.

Bryce Aiden Tyler suddenly composed himself, stood upright and straightened his waistcoat, checked his pocket watch and strode out into the hallway. "Well, Witherspoon. I doubt today people would treat other people with such disdain... even if they are slaves." Bryce frowned, "You know, I simply do not trust this strange medicine man. He could have been a charlatan and Mr. Hargreaves could have been in a gullible mood."

"But he must have found something of consequence, sir," Witherspoon commented, "Otherwise, why kill Mr. Hargreaves?"

"Indeed," Bryce stared thoughtfully, "Then, let us try to discern the manner in which one might get a body across the room without making footprints in the dust..." Bryce slumped his shoulders, now realizing the gravity of his loss.

Witherspoon said, "The clock, sir."

"The clock?" Bryce Aiden Tyler asked.

"The town clock, Sir." Witherspoon explained, "It struck the hour as you knocked that day, but then it gonged once more. However, I recall that the second gong was not an echo, nor did it sound like the town clock...it was different..."

"Do you think it could have been a firearm rapport?" Bryce asked trying to remember.

"Sir, all that I recall is that it echoed. It was a loud sound, nevertheless," Witherspoon replied.

"I believe I must seek out Mr. Tweedbottom," Bryce stated as he headed to the front door.

"Sir?" Witherspoon asked as he opened the door for Mr. Bryce Aiden Tyler.

"Yes? What is it?"" Bryce asked as he put on his gloves.

Witherspoon replied, "I know slaves are collected from all lands. I have even heard of tales from a *Bight* near the area of *Biafra.* It has been said that it is located off the western coast where the *Akan* people reside. This area is very active in slave trade. I have been told that during a routine sea voyage, half the passengers... or human-cargo... become sickly and a significant amount actually die during transport."

"Slavery is not my trade, Witherspoon," Bryce replied.

"But, sir," Witherspoon added, "What if this medicine man who spoke with Mr. Hargreaves was correct... what if it becomes easy for slave traders to capture actual colonists and force them into slavery... Slaves captured right here would not die during transport because they are already here. Perhaps that is what Mr. Hargreaves was trying to prevent. Perhaps he was working out of avuncular protective instinct once his niece Jane had arrived. Perhaps he feared she might be taken and was trying to make this colony safe for her."

Bryce popped his hat on and gave it a tap as he stepped through the front door, and said, "I don't think the slave traders are willing to kidnap their own neighbors as a fresh source of inventory for slavery. I believe those who have endured the voyage to settle in a colony here will not contribute to the theft of their loved ones just so the crown could make a profit. "

"Indeed, sir, I suppose it would depend on how lucrative the offer was, and how flexible ones morals are. It is always easiest to do nothing when evil schemes bud..." Witherspoon gave a short bow as he started to close the door behind Bryce Aiden Tyler.

Mr. Tyler turned around and faced Witherspoon as he put his hand on the door to stop it from closing. He said, "Witherspoon, earlier, Mr. Tweedbottom implied to Miss Hargreaves that I was involved somehow in her uncle's demise. I notice you possess sound insight. I would like to stroll to Mr.Tweedbottom's shop. Are you able to accompany me?"

Witherspoon looked at Bryce Aiden Tyler before he replied with, "Will you engage Mr. Tweedbottom for the purposes of righting your reputation with Miss Hargreaves? Or to confirm Mr. Hargreaves died by his own hand? Or do you believe Mr. Tweedbottom may have some knowledge of who might have, in fact, murdered Mr. Hargreaves?"

Bryce replied with a smile, "As a gentleman's gentleman, I would charge you with the responsibility to ensure that this gentleman," Bryce pointed to himself as he continued, "does not meet the same end as your previous gentleman." He took a deep breath and then added, "Why don't you accompany me and thereby discover what I shall discuss with Mr. Tweedbottom?"

9 What Just Happened?

We have learned that Bryce Aiden Tyler seeks another way to earn money and does not want to earn money from the unregulated, yet lucrative slave trade which is burgeoning in these unformed Colonies.

Likewise Jane and Polly's friendship has deepened as they both silently agree to disregard any hostilities their people may have had against each other in their homelands.　Jane has succeeded in finding accommodations for Polly as she is in a delicate state, at the moment while Jane still hunts for the truth. Meanwhile, Bryce is also making progress as he unfurls the seemingly impossible puzzle.

Unbeknownst to Jane, she is actually putting herself into danger.

10 Did You Know...

Some suspect the condiment Mayonnaise was invented in France around 1756 by the French chef working for the Duke de Richelieu.

His full name was Armand-Emmanuel Sophie Septimanie de Vignerot du Plessis, 5th Duke of Richelieu and Fronsac (25 September 1766 – 17 May 1822). He was Count of Chinon until 1788 when he succeded his father and became a Duke.

Marie Antoinette exiled him and he left Paris in 1790 for Vienna to discuss the French Revolution with her older brother, the Holy Roman Emperor

Joseph II. Before he got there, however, Joseph died and Richelieu attended the coronation of the new Emperor, Leopold II. It is said that after he defeated the British at Port Mahon, he held a feast with a new creamy egg-based sauce we know today as Mayonnaise. Some say the name came from *moyeu*, an old French word for yolk.

Others, however, argue that such a sauce must have originated in Bayonne, a town famous across Europe for its succulent hams and the sauce was called bayonnaise.

In Madrid, Spain, it was called *salsa mahonesa*

By 1838, the gourmet eatery Delmonico's in Manhattan, New York, served both a mayonnaise of lobster and also a chicken mayonnaise. It became a food of the elite patrons of fine restaurants. Mayonnaise was used in potato salads, tomato salads, and Waldorf salads. Waldorf Salad is comprised of apple, celery, walnuts, and mayonnaise. Many chefs add grapes, lemon juice, and rock salt and serve the mixture over tender lettuce leaves.

Some say the popularity of this condiment actually encouraged the spread of refrigeration units. Those who could design jars with wide openings to accommodate large spoons would dominate the market and take an elite condiment, making it available to the common worker's table.

Think about something which is being introduced as a new treat for the upper classes and create a supporting element for that thing to make it more accessible to more people. For example, mayo needs to be packaged so people can easily access it. This results in better package design. Mayo needs to be stored at a consistent temperature, so refrigeration is needed.

11 Vocabulary

In the early 1770s, before the colonies united into the United States of America, some words and terms were used, which may be explained in this section.

Akan This is a term referencing the residents of modern day West Africa, which includes Ghana. This term has been in use since around the 1690's.

Bight of Biafra, "Byht" is a term from Old English which indicates the meaning "bend, angle, corner." In this story, it references an area of land which may be shaped to be pliable and curved, narrow and long portion of the coastline in modern day West Africa. This has been in use since the 15th century. Old maps from the 1500's to 1700's indicate this region with the terms *Biafra*, *Biafara*,and *Biafares*. This could reference the modern day Cameroon, by the Niger River. It may be referenced as *Golfe du Biafra* locally. The West African "Republic of Biafra", existed from May 1967 to January 1970.

Malfeasance is a word meaning an official misconduct, a violation of a public trust or obligation. A term used since the 1690s.

Malfeasant is a person or "wrong-doer" who has done an act which is positively unlawful or wrongful. It is a person who transgresses moral or civil law. The French word *malfaisance* is translated to mean "wrongdoing".

ABOUT Wynter Sommers

Wynter Sommers is the pseudonym for an American writing team, which harnesses multiple skills in technology, research, history and education. Formally trained with a PhD in Education,

Wynter Sommers blends academic classroom experience, with corporate sophistication, and a passion for developing more effective student insights through engaging storytelling.
Wynter Sommers has a heart to inspire creativity and develop critical thinking skills, all to encourage readers to make wise choices in life.

Wynter Sommers takes each story and weaves the plot with classic gripping elements, which endure throughout repeated readings, revealing new meanings each time the story is explored. The small choices a reader makes in real life could have a lasting effect in future generations. This set of stories shows the origin of not just Bjorn Esterday and Sarah Paradise, but of their ancestors and the sort of world which was established, which unfolded in each generation until Bjorn and Sarah met.

It is rewarding to learn of heartfelt, thought provoking conversations taking place globally about the characters of these books. Should the reader be presented with extraordinary circumstances, it is the sincerest wish that they act with honor, truth and integrity to overcome obstacles in real life whilst the reader hones skills of self-reliance and collaborative teamwork despite barriers outside of the reader's control. Wynter Sommers hopes you enjoy the other ***Bjorn Esterday Was not Born Yesterday*** stories in this series.